THE

HAUNTED BOOKSHELF

T he telling or reading of ghost stories during long, dark and cold Christmas nights is a yuletide ritual which dates to at least the eighteenth century, and was once as much a part of Christmas tradition as decorating fir trees, feasting on goose and the singing of carols. During the Victorian era many magazines printed ghost stories specifically for the Christmas season. These "winter tales" did not necessarily explore Christmas themes in any manner. Rather, they were offered as an eerie pleasure to be enjoyed on Christmas eve with the family, adding a supernatural shiver to the seasonal chill.

This tradition remained strong in the British Isles (and her colonies) throughout much of the twentieth century, though in recent years it has been on the wane. Certainly, few people in Canada or the United States seem to know about it any longer. This series of small books seeks to rectify this, to revive a charming custom for the long, dark nights we all know so well here at Christmastime.

THE HAUNTED BOOKSHELF

ONE WHO SAW

ONE WHO SAW

A. M. BURRAGE

A GHOST STORY FOR CHRISTMAS
DESIGNED & DECORATED BY SETH

BIBLIOASIS

here are certain people, often well enough liked, genial souls whom one is always glad to meet, who yet have the faculty of disappearing without being missed. Crutchley must have been one of them. It wasn't until his name was casually mentioned that evening at the Storgates' that most of us remembered that we hadn't seen him about for the last year or two. It was Mrs Storgate's effort at remembering, with the help of those nearest her at table, the guests at a certain birthday party of four years since that was the cause of Crutchley's name being mentioned. And no sooner had it been mentioned than we were all laughing, because most of us had asked one another in the same breath what had become of him.

It was Jack Price who was able to supply the information.

'For the last year or two,' he said, 'he's been living very quietly with his people in Norfolk. I heard from him only the other day.'

Mrs Storgate was interested.

'I wonder why he's chosen to efface himself,' she asked of nobody in particular. 'He was rather a lamb in his way. I used to adore that shiny black hair of his which always made me think of patent leather. I believe he owed half his invitations to his hair. I told him once that he dined out on it four nights a week.'

'It's as white as the ceiling now,' Price remarked.

Having spoken he seemed to regret it, and Mrs Storgate exclaimed:

'Oh no! We're speaking of *Simon* Crutchley.'

'I mean Simon,' said Price unwillingly.

There was a faint stir of consternation, and then a woman's voice rose above the rustle and murmur.

'Oh, but it seems impossible. That sleek, blue-black hair of his! And he can't be more than thirty-five.'

Somebody said that he'd heard of people's hair going suddenly white like that after an illness. Price was asked if Simon Crutchley had been ill. The answer was Yes. A nervous breakdown? Well, it was something very like that.

A lady who turned night into day all the year round and was suspected of drinking at least as much as was good for her, sighed, and remarked that everybody nowadays suffered from nerves. Mrs Storgate said that Simon Crutchley's breakdown and the change in his appearance doubtless accounted for his having dropped out and hidden himself away in Norfolk. And then another conversational hare was started.

Instead of joining in the hunt I found myself in a brown study, playing with breadcrumbs. I had rather liked Crutchley, although he wasn't exactly one of my own kind. He was one of those quiet fellows who are said colloquially to require a lot of knowing. In social life he had always been a detached figure, standing a little aloof from his fellow-men and seeming to study them with an air of faint and inoffensive cynicism. He was a writing man, which may have accounted for his slight mannerisms, but he didn't belong to the precious, superior and rather detestable school. Everybody agreed that he was quite a good scout, and nobody troubled to read his books, which consisted mainly of historical essays.

I tried to imagine Simon Crutchley with white hair, and then I caught myself speculating on the cause of his illness or 'breakdown.' He was the last sort of fellow whom one would have expected to be knocked to pieces like that. So far from indulging in excesses he had always been something of an aesthete. He had a comfortable private income and he certainly didn't overwork. Indeed I remembered his once telling me that he took a comfortable two years over a book.

It would be hard for me to say now whether it was by accident or design that I left at the same time as Price. Our ways lay in the same direction, and while we were lingering in the hall, waiting for our hats and coats, we agreed to share a taxi. I lived in the Temple, he in John Street, Adelphi. 'I'll tell the man to drive down Villiers Street,' I said, 'and up into the Strand again by the Tivoli, and I can drop you on the way.'

In the taxi we talked about Crutchley. I began it, and I asked leading questions. Price, you see, was the only man who seemed to have heard anything of him lately, and he was now sufficiently evasive to pique my curiosity.

'It's a queer and rather terrible story,' he said at last. 'There's no secret about it, at least I'm not pledged in any way, but I don't think poor old Simon would have liked me to tell it publicly over the dinner table. For one thing, nobody would believe it, and, for another, it's rather long.

'Besides, he didn't tell me quite all. There's one bit he couldn't—or wouldn't—tell. There was just one bit he couldn't bring himself to describe to me, and I don't suppose he'll ever manage to describe it to anybody, so nobody but himself will ever have an idea of the actual *sight* which sent him off his head for six months and turned his hair as white as a tablecloth.'

'Oh,' said I, 'then it was all through something he *saw?*'

Price nodded.

'So he says. I admit it's a pretty incredible sort of story—yet somehow Simon Crutchley isn't the sort to imagine things. And after all, something obviously did happen to him. I'll tell you his story if you like. The night's young. Come into my place and have a drink, if you will.'

I thanked him and said that I would. He turned towards me and let a hand fall on my knee.

'Mind you,' he said, 'this is Crutchley's own story. If you don't believe it I don't want you to go about thinking that I'm a liar. I'm not responsible for the truth of it; I'm only just passing it on. In a way I hope it isn't true. It isn't comfortable to think that such things may happen— *do* happen.'

Twenty minutes later, when we were sitting in the snug little library in Price's flat he told me his story, or, rather, Crutchley's. This is it.

You know the sort of work Crutchley used to do? If you don't, you at least know Stevenson's 'Memories and Portraits,' and Crutchley worked with that sort of material. His study of Margaret of Anjou, by the way, is considered a classic in certain highbrow circles.

You will remember that Joan of Arc was very much in the air two or three years back. It was before Bernard Shaw's play was produced, but her recent canonization had just reminded the world that she was perhaps the greatest woman in history. It may have been this revival of interest in her which decided Crutchley to make her the subject of one of his historical portraits. He'd already treated Villon and Abelard and Heloise, and as soon as he'd decided on St Joan he went over to France to work, so to say, on the spot.

Crutchley always did his job conscientiously, using his own deductive faculties only for bridging the gaps in straight history. He went first to Domrémy, where the Maid was born, followed the old trail of that fifteenth-century campaign across

France, and of course his journey ended inevitably at Rouen, where English spite and French cowardice burned her in the market-place.

I don't know if you know Rouen? Tourists don't stay there very much. They visit, but they don't stay. They come and hurry round the cathedral, gape at the statue of Joan of Arc in the Place de la Pucelle, throw a victorious smile at Napoleon Buonaparte galloping his bronze horse on a pedestal in the square, and rush on to Paris or back to one of the Channel ports. Rouen being half-way between Paris and the coast the typical English tourist finds that he can 'do' the place without sleeping in it.

Crutchley liked Rouen. It suited him. It is much more sober and austere than most of the French towns. It goes to bed early, and you don't have sex flaunted before you wherever you look. You find there an atmosphere like that of our own cathedral cities, and there is a great deal more to see than ever the one-day tourist imagines. Crutchley decided to stay on in the town and finish there his paper on Joan of Arc.

He found an hotel practically undiscovered by English and Americans—l'Hôtel d'Avignon. It stands half-way down one of those narrow old-world streets, quite near the Gare de la Rue Jeanne d'Arc. A single tramline runs through the narrow street in front of its unpretentious façade, and to enter you must pass a narrow archway, and through a winter garden littered with tables and chairs, to a somewhat impressive main entrance with statuary on either side of the great glass-panelled doors.

Crutchley found the place by accident on his first day and took *déjeuner* in the

great tapestried *salle à manger*. The food was good, and he found that the chef had a gift for *sole normande*. Out of curiosity he asked to see some of the bedrooms.

It was a hotel where many ate but few slept. At that time of the year many rooms were vacant on the first floor. He followed a chambermaid up the first flight of stairs and looked out through a door which he found open at the top. To his surprise he found that it gave entrance to a garden on the same level. The hotel, parts of which were hundreds of years old, had been built on the face of a steep hill, and the little garden thus stood a storey above the level of the street in front.

This garden was sunk deep in a hollow square, with the walls of the hotel rising high all around it. Three rows of shuttered windows looked out upon an open space which never saw the sun. For that obvious reason there had been no attempt to grow flowers, but one or two ferns had sprung up and a few small tenacious plants had attached themselves to a rockery. The soil was covered with loose gravel, and in the middle there grew a great plane tree which thrust its crest above the roof-tops so that, as seen by the birds, it must have looked as if it were growing in a great lidless box. To imagine the complete quietude of the spot one has only to remember how an enclosed square in one of the Inns of Court shuts out the noise of traffic from some of the busiest streets in the world. It did not occur to Crutchley that there may be something unhealthy about an open space shut out entirely from the sun. Some decrepit garden seats were ranged around the borders, and the plane tree hid most of the sky, sheltering the little enclosure like a great umbrella. Crutchley told me that he mistook silence and deathly stillness for peace, and decided that here was the very spot for him to write his version of the story of Jeanne d'Arc. He took a bedroom on the same level, whose high, shuttered windows looked out on to the still garden square; and next day he took a writing-pad and a fountain-pen to one of the faded green seats and tried to start work.

From what he told me it wasn't a very successful attempt. The unnatural silence of the place bred in him an indefinable restlessness. It seemed to him that he sat more in twilight than in shade. He knew that a fresh wind was blowing, but it won not the least responsive whisper from the garden. The ferns might have been water-plants in an aquarium, so still they were. Sunlight, which burnished the blue sky, struck through the leaves of the plane tree, but it painted only the top of one of the walls high above his head. Crutchley frankly admitted that the place got on his nerves, and that it was a relief to go out and hear the friendly noise of the trams, and see the people drinking outside cafés and the little boys fishing for roach among the barges on the banks of the Seine.

He made several attempts to work in the garden, but they were all fruitless, and he took to working in his bedroom. He confessed to me that, even in the afternoon, he felt that there was something uncanny about the place. There's nothing in that. Many people would have felt the same; and Crutchley, although he had no definite belief in the supernatural, had had one or two minor experiences in his lifetime—too trifling, he said, to be worth recording—but teasing enough in their way, and of great interest to himself. Yet he had always smiled politely when ardent spiritualists had told him that he was 'susceptible.' He began by feeling vaguely that there was something 'wrong,' in the psychical sense, with the garden. It was like a faint, unseizable, but disagreeable odour. He told me that he did not let it trouble him greatly. He wanted to work, and when he found that 'it' would not let him work in the garden, he removed himself and his writing materials to his room.

Crutchley had been five days at the hotel when something strange happened. It was his custom to undress in the dark, because his windows were overlooked by a dozen others and, by first of all turning off the light, he was saved from drawing the great shutters. That night he was smoking while he undressed, and when he was in his pyjamas he went to one of the open windows to throw out the stub of his cigarette. Having done so he lingered, looking out.

The usual unnatural stillness brooded over the garden square, intensified now by the spell of the night. Somewhere in the sky the moon was shining, and a few stray silver beams dappled the top of the north wall. The plane tree stood like a living thing entranced. Not one of its lower branches stirred, and its leaves might have been carved out of jade. Just enough light filtered from the sky to make the features of the garden faintly visible. Crutchley looked where his cigarette had fallen and now lay like a glow-worm, and raised his eyes to one of the long green decrepit seats. With a faint, unreasonable thrill and a cold tingling of the nostrils he realized that somebody was sitting there.

As his eyes grew more used to the darkness the huddled form took the shape of a woman. She sat with her head turned away, one arm thrown along the sloping back of the seat, and her face resting against it. He said that her attitude was one of extreme dejection, of abject and complete despair.

Crutchley, you must understand, couldn't see her at all clearly, although she was not a dozen yards distant. Her dress was dark, but he could make out none of its details save that something like a flimsy scarf or thick veil trailed over the shoulder nearest him. He stood watching her, pricked by a vague sense of pity and conscious that, if she looked up, he would hardly be visible to her beyond the window, and that, in any event, the still glowing stub of cigarette would explain his presence.

But she did not look up, she did not move at all while Crutchley stood watching. So still she was that it was hard for him to realize that she breathed. She seemed to have fallen completely under the spell of the garden in which nothing ever stirred, and the scene before Crutchley's eyes might have been a nocturnal picture painted in oils.

Of course he made a guess or two about her. At the sight of anything unusual one's subconscious mind immediately begins to speculate and to suggest theories. Here, thought Crutchley, was a woman with some great sorrow, who, before retiring to her room had come to sit in this quiet garden, and there, under the stars, had given way to her despair.

I don't know how long Crutchley stood there, but probably it wasn't for many seconds. Thought is swift and time is slow when one stands still watching a motionless scene. He owned that his curiosity was deeply intrigued, and it was intrigued in a somewhat unusual way. He found himself desiring less to know the reason of her despair than to see her face. He had a definite and urgent temptation to go out and look at her, to use force if necessary in turning her face so that he might look into her eyes.

If you knew Crutchley at all well you must know that he was something more than ordinarily conventional. He concerned himself not only with what a gentleman ought to do but with what a gentleman ought to think. Thus when he came to realize that he was not only spying upon a strange woman's grief, but actually feeling tempted to force himself upon her and stare into eyes which he guessed were blinded by tears, it was sufficient to tear him away from the window and send him padding across the floor to the high bed at the far end of the room.

But he made no effort to sleep. He lay listening, waiting for a sound from the other side of those windows. In that silence he knew he must hear the least sound outside. But for ten minutes he listened in vain, picturing to himself the woman still rigid in the same posture of despair. Presently he could bear it no longer. He jumped out of bed and went once more to the window. He told himself that it was human pity which drove him there. He walked heavily on his bare feet and he coughed. He made as much noise as he was reasonably able to make, hoping that she would hear and bestir herself. But when he reached the open window and looked out the seat was empty.

Crutchley stared at the empty seat, not quite crediting the evidence of his eyes. You see, according to his account, she couldn't have touched that loose gravel with her foot without making a distinct sound, and to re-enter the hotel she must have opened a door with creaking hinges and a noisy latch. Yet he had heard nothing, and the garden was empty. Next morning he even tried the experiment of walking on tiptoe across the garden to see if it could be done in utter silence, and he was satisfied that it could not. Even an old grey cat, which he found blinking on a window ledge, made the gravel clink under its pads when he called it to him to be stroked.

Well, he slept indifferently that night, and in the morning, when the chambermaid came in, he asked her who was the sad-looking lady whom he had seen sitting at night in the garden.

The chambermaid turned towards the window, and he saw a rapid movement of her right hand. It was done very quickly and surreptitiously, just the touch of a forefinger on her brow and a rapid fumbling of fingers at her breast, but he knew that she had made the Sign of the Cross.

'There is no lady staying in the house,' she said with her back towards him. 'Monsieur has been mistaken. Will Monsieur take coffee or the English tea?'

Crutchley knew very well what that girl's gesture meant. He had mentioned something which she held to be unholy, and the look on her face when she turned it once more in his direction warned him that it would be useless to question her. He had a pretty restless day, doing little or no work. You mustn't think that he already regarded the experience as a supernatural one, although he was quite well aware of what was in the mind of the chambermaid; but it was macabre, it belonged to the realm of the seemingly inexplicable which was no satisfaction to him to dismiss as merely 'queer.'

Crutchley spoke the French of the average educated Englishman, and the only other person in the house who spoke English was the head waiter, who had spent some years in London. His English was probably at least as good as Crutchley's French, and he enjoyed the opportunity of airing it. He was in appearance a true Norman, tall, dark, and distinguished looking. One sees his type in certain English families which can truthfully boast of Norman ancestry. It was at *déjeuner* when he approached Crutchley, and, having handed him the wine list, bent over him confidentially.

'Are you quite comfortable in your room, sir?' he ventured.

'Oh, quite, thank you,' Crutchley answered briefly.

'There is a very nice room in the front, sir. Quite so big, and then there is the sun. Perhaps you like it better, sir?'

'No, thanks,' said Crutchley, 'I shouldn't get a wink of sleep. You see, none of your motor-traffic seems to be equipped with silencers, and with trams, motor-horns, and market carts bumping over the cobbles I should never have any peace.'

The waiter said no more, merely bowing, but he looked disappointed. He managed to convey by a look that he had Monsieur's welfare at heart, but that Monsieur doubtless knew best and must please himself.

'I believe I'm on the trail of something queer,' Crutchley thought. 'That chambermaid's been talking to Pierre. I wonder what's wrong or what they think is wrong.'

He re-opened the subject when the waiter returned to him with a half-bottle of white wine.

'Why do you wish me to change my room, Pierre?'

'I do not wish Monsieur to change his room if he is satisfied.'

'When I am not satisfied I say so. Why did you think I might not be?'

'I wish Monsieur to be more comfortable. There is no sun behind the house. It is better to be where the sun comes sometimes. Besides, I think Monsieur is one who sees.'

This seemed cryptic, but Crutchley let it go. Pierre had duties to attend to, and, besides, Crutchley did not feel inclined to discuss with the waiter the lady he had seen in the garden on the preceding night.

During the afternoon and evening he tried to work, but he fought only a series of losing battles against distraction. He was as incapable of concentration as a boy in love. He knew—and he was angry with himself because he knew—that he was eking out his patience until night came, in the hope of seeing once more that still figure of despair in the garden.

Of course, I don't pretend to understand the nature of the attraction, nor was Crutchley able to explain it to me. But he told me that he couldn't keep his thoughts off the face which had been turned away from him. Imagination drew for him a succession of pictures, all of an unearthly beauty, such pictures as he had never before conceived. His mind, over which he now seemed to have only an imperfect control, exercised its new creative faculty all that afternoon and evening. Long before the hour of dinner he had decided that if she came to the garden he must see her face and thus end this long torment of speculation.

He went to his room that night at eleven o'clock, and he did not undress, but sat and smoked in an armchair beside his bed. From that position he could only see through the window the lighted windows of other rooms across the square of garden shining through the leaves of the plane tree. Towards midnight the last lights died out and the last distant murmur of voices died away. Then he got up and went softly across the room.

Before he reached the window he knew instinctively that he would see her sitting in the same place and in the same attitude of woe, and his eagerness was mingled with an indescribable fear. He seemed to hear a cry of warning from the honest workaday world into which he had been born—a world which he now seemed strangely to be leaving. He said that it was like starting on a voyage, feeling no motion from the ship, and then being suddenly aware of a spreading space of water between the vessel and the quay.

That night the invisible moon threw stronger beams upon the top of the north wall, and the stars burned brighter in a clearer sky. There was a little more light in the well of the garden than there had been on the preceding night, and on the seat that figure of tragic desolation was limned more clearly. The pose, the arrangement of the woman's garments, were the same in every detail, from the least fold to the wisp of veil which fell over her right shoulder. For he now saw that it was a veil, and guessed that it covered the face which was still turned from him. He was shaken, dragged in opposite directions by unreasonable dread and still more unreasonable curiosity. And while he stood looking, the palms of his hands grew wet and his mouth grew dry.

He was well nigh helpless. His spirit struggled within him like a caged bird, longing to fly to her. That still figure was magnetic in some mighty sense which he had never realized before. It was hypnotic without needing to use its eyes. And presently Crutchley spoke to it for the first time, whispering through the open window across the intervening space of gloom.

'Madame,' he pleaded, 'look at me.'

The figure did not more. It might have been cast in bronze or carved out of stone.

'Oh, Madame,' he whispered, 'let me see your face!'

Still there was no sound nor movement, but in his heart he heard the answer.

'So, then, I must come to you,' he heard himself say softly; and he groped for the door of his room.

Outside, a little way down the corridor, was one of the doors leading into the enclosed garden. Crutchley had taken but a step or two when a figure loomed up before him, his nerves were jerked like a hooked fish, and he uttered an involuntary cry of fear. Then came the click of an electric light switch, a globe overhead sprang alight, and he found himself confronted by Pierre the head waiter. Pierre barred the way and he spoke sternly, almost menacingly.

'Where are you going, sir?'

'What the devil has that got to do with you?' Crutchley demanded fiercely.

'The devil, eh? *Bien*, Monsieur, I think perhaps he have something to do with it. You will have the goodness, please, to return to your room. No, not the room which you have left, sir—that is not a good room—but come with me and I shall show you another.'

The waiter was keeping him from her. Crutchley turned upon him with a gesture of ferocity.

'What do you mean by interfering with me? This is not a prison or an asylum. I am going into the garden for a breath of air before I go to sleep.'

'That, sir, is impossible,' the waiter answered him. 'The air of the garden is not good at night. Besides, the doors are locked and the patron have the keys.'

Crutchley stared at him for a moment in silent fury.

'You are insolent,' he said. 'Tomorrow I shall report you. Do you take me for a thief because I leave my room at midnight? Never mind! I can reach the garden from my window.'

In an instant the waiter had him by the arm, holding him powerless in a grip known to wrestlers.

'Monsieur,' he said in a voice grown softer and more respectful, 'the *bon Dieu* has sent me to save you. I have wait tonight because I know you must try to enter the garden. Have I your permission to enter your room with you and speak with you a little while?'

Crutchley laughed out in angry impotence.

'This is Bedlam,' he said. 'Oh, come, if you must.'

Back in his room, with the waiter treading close upon his heels, Crutchley went straight to the window and looked out. The seat was empty.

'I do not think that she is there,' said the waiter softly, 'because I am here and I do not see. Monsieur is one who sees, as I tell him this morning, but he will not see her when he is with one who does not see.'

Crutchley turned upon the man impatiently.

'What are you talking about?' he demanded. 'Who is she?'

'Who she is, I cannot say.' The waiter blessed himself with quick, nervous fingers. 'But who she *was* I can perhaps tell Monsieur.'

Crutchley understood, almost without surprise, but with a sudden clamouring of fear.

'Do you mean,' he asked, 'that she is what we call a ghost, an apparition—'

'It matters not what one calls her, Monsieur. She is here sometimes for certain who are able to see her. Monsieur wishes very much to see her face. Monsieur must not see it. There was one who look five years ago, and another perhaps seven, eight. The first he make die after two, three days; the other, he is still mad. That is why I come to save you, Monsieur.'

Crutchley was now entirely back in his own world. That hidden face had lost its fascination for him, and he felt only the primeval dread which has its roots deep down in every one of us. He sat down on the bed, trying to keep his lips from twitching, and let the waiter talk.

'You asked Yvonne this morning, sir, who is the lady in the garden. And Yvonne guess, and she come and tell me, for all of us know of her. Monsieur, it all happened a long time ago—perhaps fifty—sixty years. There was in this town a notary of the name Lebrun. And in a village half-way from here to Dieppe is a *grand château* in which there live a lady, *une jeune fille*, with her father and her mother. And the lady was very beautiful but not very good, Monsieur.

'Well, M. Lebrun, he fall in love with her. I think she love him, too—better as all the others. So he make application for her hand, but she was aristocrat and he was *bourgeois*, and besides he had not very much money, so the application was refused! And they find her another husband whom she love not, and she find herself someone else, and there is divorce. And she have many lovers, for she was very beautiful; but not good. For ten years—more, perhaps—she use her beauty to make slaves of men. And one, he made kill himself because of her, but she did not mind. And all the time M. Lebrun stayed single, because he could not love another woman.

'But at last this lady, she have a dreadful accident. It is a lamp which blow up and hurt her face. In those days the surgeons did not know how to make new features. It was dreadful, Monsieur. She had been so lovely, and now she have nothing left except just the eyes. And she go about wearing a long, thick veil, because she have become terrible to see. And her lovers, they no longer love, and she have no husband because she have been divorce.

'So M. Lebrun, he write to her father, and once more he make offer for her hand. And her father, he is willing, because now she is no longer very young, and she is terrible to see. But her father, he was a man of honour, and he insist that M. Lebrun must see her face before he decide if he still wish her in marriage. So a meeting is arrange and her father and her mother bring her to this hotel, and M. Lebrun he come to see them here.

'The lady come with them wearing her thick veil. She insist to see M. Lebrun alone, so she wait out there in the garden, and when he come they bring him to her.

'Monsieur, I do not know what her face was like, and nobody know what pass between him and her in that garden there. Love is not always what we think it. Perhaps M. Lebrun think all the time that his love go deeper than her beauty, and when he see her dreadful changed face he find out the truth. Perhaps when she put aside the veil she see that he flinch. I only say perhaps, because nobody know. But M. Lebrun he walk out alone, and the lady stay sitting on the seat. And presently her parents come, but she does not speak or move. And they find in her hand a little empty bottle, Monsieur . . .

'All her life she have live for love, for admiration, and M. Lebrun, he is the last of her lovers, and when he no longer love it is for her the end of everything. She have bring the bottle with her in case her last lover love her no more. That is all, Monsieur. It happen many years ago, and if there is more of the story one does not remember it today. And now perhaps Monsieur understands why it would be best for him to sleep tonight in a front room, and change his hotel tomorrow.'

Crutchley sat listening and staring. He felt faint and sick.

'But why does she—come back?' he managed to ask.

The head waiter shrugged his shoulders.

'How should we know, Monsieur? She is a thing of evil. When her face was lovely, while she live, she use it to destroy men. Now she still use it to destroy—but otherwise. She have some great evil power which draw those who can see her. They feel they must not rest until they have looked upon her face. And, Monsieur, that face is not good to look upon.'

I had listened all this while to Price's version of Crutchley's story without making any comment, but now he paused for so long that at last I said:

'Well, that can't be all.'

Price was filling a pipe with an air of preoccupation.

'No,' he said, 'it isn't quite all. I wish it were. Crutchley was scared, and he had the sense to change to a room in the front of the house, and to clear out altogether next day. He paid his bill, and made Pierre a good-sized present in money. Having done that, he found that he hadn't quite enough money to get home with, and he'd used his last letter of credit. So he telegraphed for more, meaning to catch the night boat from Havre.

'Well, you can guess what happened. The wired money order didn't arrive in time, and he was compelled to stay another night in Rouen. He went to another hotel.

'All that day he could think of nothing else but that immobile figure of despair which he had seen on the seat. I imagine that if you or I had seen something which we believed to be a ghost we should find difficulty in concentrating our minds on anything else for some while afterwards.

'The horror of the thing had a fascination for Crutchley, and when night fell he began to ask himself if she were still there, hiding her face in that dark and silent garden. And he began to ask himself: 'Why shouldn't I go and see? It could not harm me just to look once, and quickly, and from a distance.'

'He didn't realize that she was calling him, drawing him to her through the lighted streets. Well, he walked round to the Hôtel d'Avignon. People were still sitting at the little tables under the glass roof, but he did not see Pierre. He walked

straight on and through the swing doors, as if he were still staying in the house, and nobody noticed him. He climbed the stairs and went to one of the doors which opened out into the high enclosed garden behind. He found it on the latch, opened it softly and looked out. Then he stood, staring in horror and fascination at that which was on the seat.

'He was lost then, and he knew it. The power was too strong for him. He went to her step by step, as powerless to hold himself back as a needle before a magnet or a moth before a flame. And he bent over her . . .

'And here is the part that Crutchley can't really describe. It was painful to see him straining and groping after words, as if he were trying to speak in some strange language. There aren't really any words, I suppose. But he told me that it wasn't just that—that there weren't any features left. It was something much worse and much more subtle than that. And—oh, something happened, I know, before his senses left him. Poor devil, he couldn't tell me. He's getting better, as I told you, but his nerves are still in shreds and he's got one or two peculiar aversions.'

'What are they?' I asked.

'He can't bear to be touched, or to hear anybody laugh.'

lfred McLelland Burrage (1889–1956) was a prolific British writer remembered most fondly for his tales of horror. His two most famous collections are *Some Ghost Stories* (1927) and *Someone in the Room* (1931, written under the pseudonym "Ex-Private X"). Burrage's short fiction has been widely anthologized.

eth is the cartoonist behind the comic-book series *Palookaville*, which started in the stone age as a pamphlet and is now a semi-annual hardcover. His comics have appeared in the *New York Times Magazine*, *Best American Comics*, and *McSweeney's Quarterly*. His illustrations have appeared in numerous publications including the cover of the *New Yorker*, the *Walrus*, and *Canadian Notes & Queries*. He is the subject of a recent documentary from the National Film board of Canada, *Seth's Dominion*.

Seth lives in Guelph, Ontario, with his wife Tania and their two cats in an old house he has named "Inkwell's End."

Publisher's Note: 'One Who Saw' was first published in the 1931 collection *Someone in the Room*, and has been widely anthologized since.

Illustrations and design © Seth, 2015

Library and Archives Canada Cataloguing in Publication

Burrage, Alfred McLelland, author
One who saw / A.M. Burrage ; Seth, illustrator.

(Christmas ghost stories)
Issued in print and electronic formats.
ISBN 978-1-77196-066-3 (paperback)
--ISBN 978-1-77196-093-9 (epub)

I. Seth, 1962-, illustrator II. Title.

PR6003.U63O54 2015   823'.912   C2015-906732-4
                                    C2015-906733-2

Readied for the press by Daniel Wells
Illustrated and Designed by Seth
Copy-edited by Emily Donaldson
Typeset by Chris Andrechek

PRINTED AND BOUND IN CHINA